Shelley
the Sherbet
Fairy

by Daisy Meadows

ORCHARD

www.rainbowmagic.co.uk

Jack Frost's Spell

Give me candy! Give me sweets!
Give me sticky, fizzy treats!
Lollipops and fudge so yummy –
Bring them here to fill my tummy.

Monica, I'll steal from you.
Gabby, Lisa, Shelley too.
I will build a sweetie shop,
So I can eat until I pop!

Contents

An Extra Present

Rachel Walker was sitting at the bottom of the stairs in her best friend Kirsty Tate's house, doing up her party shoes.

"It's kind of your schoolfriend to invite me to her birthday party," said Rachel.

"Anna knows how excited I am to have you staying with me for a whole week," Kirsty said, smiling. "She's looking forward to meeting you."

Rachel jumped to her feet and smoothed down her party dress.

"I'm ready," she said. "Let's go."

Kirsty put their presents for Anna into a bag and then opened the front door. To her surprise, she saw her Aunt Harri standing there.

"Oh!" said Aunt Harri. "That's lucky – I was just about to knock. Goodness me, you two look smart."

"We're on our way to my friend Anna Goldman's birthday

party," Kirsty explained.

"I know," said Aunt Harri. "Actually, I'm here to give you a lift to the party. You see, Anna has won a Candy Land Helping Hands award, and I was hoping

that you would present it to her."

Kirsty clapped her hands together in delight.

"This will be a really perfect birthday surprise for Anna," she said. "She has raised lots of money for the Wetherbury Children's Hospital."

Aunt Harri worked at the Candy Land sweet factory. She was in charge of organising the Helping Hands awards, which were special parcels of sweets for local children who did helpful things around the community. Kirsty and Rachel had been helping her to present the awards all week.

Kirsty and Rachel said goodbye to Mr and Mrs Tate, and then jumped into Aunt Harri's Candy Land van. It didn't take long to reach the Wetherbury village hall.

"Wow, the village hall looks amazing," said Kirsty.

Rachel looked up too. Colourful balloons were tied to the hall railings and there were more around the doorway. A huge banner above the door said HAPPY BIRTHDAY, ANNA!

"I'm good friends with Anna's mum,"
said Aunt Harri. "We got up early
this morning and came here to do the
decorations. I'm still shaking the sparkles
out of my hair!"

The girls laughed as they got out of the van. Aunt Harri stayed in her seat.

"Aren't you coming in?" Kirsty asked.

"I'll be back soon," said Aunt Harri. "First I'm going to Candy Land to pick up Anna's cake. Her mum told me that her favourite sweet is sherbet, so her Helping Hand award  is a special sherbet birthday cake. I'll bring it here for the end of the party, and you can both help me to surprise Anna."

As soon as the girls heard the word 'sherbet', they exchanged a worried

glance. Luckily, Aunt Harri didn't notice.
The girls waved goodbye as she drove
off. Then they walked up the path
towards the hall, carrying the present bag
between them.

"Oh dear, I'd forgotten how much
Anna likes sherbet," said Kirsty in a low
voice. "I hope her cake won't be ruined
by Jack Frost and his naughty goblins."

Sweets had been going wrong ever

since Jack Frost and his goblins had
stolen the magical objects from the
Candy Land Fairies. Rachel and
Kirsty had helped their fairy friends to
get three of the objects back, but there
was still one missing.

Rachel looked down at the bag of
presents and stopped in her tracks.

"Kirsty," she said in an urgent whisper. "Look at that!"

The bag of birthday presents was glowing as if a ray of sunshine was trapped inside. Feeling bubbly with excitement, Rachel and Kirsty peered inside. To their delight, they saw Shelley

the Sherbet Fairy sitting on top of a sparkly birthday bow.

Shelley looked summery in her sunshine-yellow dress, with a beautiful pink rose in her brown hair. She fluttered out of the bag and flitted back and forth between the girls.

"Rachel and Kirsty, I have to get my magical sherbet straw back from Jack Frost," she said in an urgent voice. "The Harvest Feast is today. Please, will you help me?"

A Fizzy Mess

"We'll do everything we can to help,"
said Rachel.

On the first day of Rachel's visit to
Wetherbury, Monica the Marshmallow
Fairy had whisked the girls away to the
Sweet Factory in Fairyland. She had
introduced them to Gabby the Bubble
Gum Fairy, Lisa the Jelly Bean Fairy and
Shelley the Sherbet Fairy.

The Candy Land Fairies had just invited the girls to the Harvest Feast, when there was a commotion in the orchard. Jack Frost and his goblins were shaking sweets off the trees. In the confusion, they stole four sparkly magical sweets from the Candy Land Fairies. Jack Frost wanted lots and lots of sweets for the new sweet shop at his Ice Castle, but instead of selling sweets, he was going to eat them all himself.

Without their special sweets, the fairies couldn't make sure that all sweets in Fairyland and the human world were sweet and delicious. Rachel and Kirsty had promised to help get them all back. They had found three, so now they just had to help Shelley get her magical sherbet straw back.

Just then, the door of the village hall started to open.

"Quickly, hide in my bag," said Kirsty.

Shelley swooped into Kirsty's shoulder bag just in time. The door opened and a man came out carrying a bunch of balloons.

"Hi, Mr Goldman," said Kirsty.

"Hello, Kirsty," said Mr Goldman. "Please go in and find Anna. I'm just adding a few more balloons to the railings."

The girls walked in and saw balloons swirling in the air. Most of the children in the hall were jumping up and down, batting the balloons around.

"Look, there are the other Helping Hands award

winners," said Rachel.

Ori, Olivia, Tal and a girl with blonde curls were bouncing around on hoppers, giggling as they bumped into each other.

"Kirsty!" exclaimed the blonde girl.

She jumped off her hopper and ran over to hug Kirsty. Then she turned to Rachel.

"You must be Rachel," she said, smiling. "I've heard so much about you. I'm Anna. It's really great to meet you."

"Thanks for inviting me," said Rachel. "I love all the balloons! The food looks amazing too."

There was a long refreshment table at the side of the room. The tablecloth was decorated with rockets, spaceships, planets and shooting stars. There were enormous bowls filled with sherbet lemons and flying saucers.

"My mum got lots of my favourite sherbet sweets, but we're not allowed to eat them until later," said Anna. "I can hardly wait!"

Just then, the music stopped and Anna's mum clapped her hands together.

"It's time for the first game," she said. "Everyone gather round for pass the parcel."

As soon as everyone was sitting in a circle, Mrs Goldman started playing the music. A bulky package was passed around the circle, and when the music stopped, Rachel was holding the parcel. Eagerly, she ripped open the top layer and found a packet of sherbet popping candy.

"Oh yum, I love popping candy," she said. "Would everyone like some?"

She opened the packet and the popping candy fizzed right out, spilling a raspberry-coloured mess across the floor.

"Oh no," said Rachel with a groan. "It looks as if there is something wrong with the sherbet after all."

She exchanged a worried glance with Kirsty.

"I'll help you clean it up," said Kirsty,

jumping to her feet.

The girls wiped up the sherbet mess, talking in low voices.

"We can't let Aunt Harri bring the cake in here yet," said Rachel. "Not until we can find Shelley's magical sherbet straw and take it back from Jack Frost and the goblins."

"We haven't got much time," said Kirsty.

Just then, they heard a faint giggle. Then there was an excited squeal, followed by another giggle.

"It's coming from under the refreshment table," Rachel said.

The girls peered under the tablecloth and saw four green, knobbly faces.

"Goblins!" they exclaimed.

Through the Keyhole

The goblins were cramming green
sherbet sweets into their mouths. Their
cheeks were bulging, and green sherbet
was foaming out of their mouths and
dribbling down their chins. The tallest
goblin waved a sherbet straw, and a new
pile of sweets appeared in front of him.

Kirsty felt her shoulder bag move, and

looked down to see Shelley peeping out.

"That's my magical sherbet straw,"
she said with an excited gasp. "Oh my
goodness, I'm so happy that we've found
it – but I have no idea how we are going
to get it back!"

The other children were still busy
playing pass the parcel, and Mr and Mrs
Goldman were watching the game.

"Let's go and find a safe place where
you can turn us into fairies," Rachel
suggested. "Then we will have a chance
of getting close to the magical sherbet
straw without the goblins spotting us."

"Yes, good thinking," said Kirsty.
"How about the garden at the back of
the village hall?"

Rachel nodded, and Shelley ducked
down inside the bag again. Then the girls

slipped out of the back door and into the
garden. No one was watching, so Kirsty
opened her bag and Shelley fluttered out.

"There's no time to lose," she said,
waving her wand.

"Jack Frost's goblins cannot scare me.
I'm a brave and fearless fairy!
Fly with me, do not delay.
We'll find the straw and save the day!"

35

A fountain of fizzing sparkles burst
from Shelley's wand and showered the
girls in sparkling fairy dust. They felt
their skin tingling as they shrank to fairy
size. Delicate pastel wings unfurled on
their backs, and the sweet scent of sherbet
filled the air. Rachel and Kirsty twirled
upwards, fluttering their wings in delight
at being fairies again.

"Let's go back inside the hall," said
Shelley, taking their hands.

Now that they were small, they were
able to swoop through the gap under the
back door. They zoomed back into the

hall, flying high among the balloons and
birthday banners. When they were above
the refreshment table, they hovered and
exchanged determined looks.

"Let's dive down and take the goblins
by surprise," said Kirsty. "Maybe we can

get the magical sherbet straw before they realise what's going on."

Side by side, the three fairies whooshed under the tablecloth and flew towards the tallest goblin. He jumped up in a panic and banged his head on the underneath of the table.

"Fairies!" he squawked, staggering sideways. "Shoo! Go away!"

The other goblins scrambled away, stumbling over the sherbet sweets they had dropped. One of them clutched at the tablecloth and fell over. *CRASH!* The bowls of sweets were pulled down

from the refreshment table, sending even more sherbets spilling on to the floor. The fairies peered out from under the table. A green, fizzy mess was foaming across the village hall towards the children, who giggled and jumped around when they saw it.

"They think it's another bit of party fun," said Kirsty.

"Poor Mr and Mrs Goldman," said Rachel.

Anna's parents were trying to clear up the mess, but it was getting worse.

"Where have the goblins gone?" asked Shelley suddenly.

There was no sign of Jack Frost's naughty helpers, but then Kirsty spotted some big footprints in the green sherbet mess.

"Those are goblin prints," she said. "Come on, if we follow them they should lead us straight to the goblins – and the magical sherbet straw."

The fairies followed the footprints out of the village hall main room and across the corridor towards a door labelled *Soft Play*. There wasn't a big enough gap under the door for them to get through, but Rachel pointed at the keyhole.

"We should be able to squeeze through there," she said. "It's made for an old-fashioned key."

She put her head into the keyhole and wriggled through.

Soft Play Party

When Rachel pulled herself out of the keyhole, she heard the squeals, squawks and cackles of the goblins. They were leaping around on the spongy mats, bouncy slide and soft climbing frame. The goblin with the sherbet straw was hurling brightly coloured sponge balls at the others. Kirsty and Shelley popped through the keyhole after Rachel.

"I think that the fizzy sherbets have made the goblins go completely fizzy with excitement," said Shelley. "I wonder if the tallest goblin will put my magical straw down while he plays."

The fairies watched the tallest goblin carefully, but he seemed to be clutching the straw more tightly than ever.

"How are we ever going to get it back?" Kirsty asked.

Rachel suddenly felt full of fizzy excitement herself.

"I've got an idea," she said. "Maybe
we can use those sponge balls to make
him drop the straw."

Together, the three fairies lifted one of
the balls and aimed it at the goblin.

"Ready, steady, GO!" said Rachel.

Together, they threw the ball at the
goblin, but he dodged sideways and it
missed. They flew down to get another

one, but they missed again.

"We have to keep trying," said Shelley, panting from the effort.

Over and over again, faster and faster, the fairies hurled the soft balls with all their might towards the goblin. But he was just too quick for them.

"This is fun!" he said, cackling with horrible laughter. "Is this what birthday parties are like?"

"I've always wanted to be invited to a birthday party," said another goblin. "Let me have a go."

Kirsty turned to Rachel and Shelley.

"This isn't working," she said. "But I think I know what we should do. If these goblins want a party, let's give them a party. First we will need to be human again. Then we'll need a wrapped-up parcel and some music."

With a wave of Shelley's wand, Rachel and Kirsty were back to their normal size. A large parcel appeared in Kirsty's arms, and Rachel found herself holding the remote control for the stereo in the corner. Shelley quickly tucked herself into Kirsty's bag.

"Does anyone want to learn how to

play pass the parcel?" asked Kirsty in a loud voice. "It's one of the best birthday party games, I think."

Three of the goblins raced over to her at once, jumping up and down in excitement.

"Sit down in a circle," said Kirsty, glancing at the fourth goblin, who was holding the magical sherbet straw. "What about you? Aren't you going to join in the fun?"

"If I have to," said the goblin in a grumpy voice.

He joined the circle, still clutching

the magical sherbet straw in his hand.
Rachel and Kirsty sat down too. Kirsty
quickly explained the rules, and then
Rachel pressed the play button and the
music began.

The goblins
snatched the parcel
from each other
as they passed
it around, and
held on to it for
as long as they
could. When the
music stopped, the
goblin who was holding

the parcel squealed with excitement.
He unwrapped the first layer and found
some green goblin stickers.

All the other goblins said "Oooh" and

"Ahhh", leaning over and peering at the stickers. The goblin clutched them to his chest, his eyes sparkling.

"This is the best game ever," he said.

The tallest goblin gazed at the stickers but said nothing. The music started again, and next it was the shortest goblin's turn to unwrap a layer. Gleefully, he pulled out a pencil with a wobbly goblin on top. The tallest goblin stared at it so hard that his eyes bulged.

Next, the music stopped on the tallest goblin's turn. He was so excited to find out what his prize would be that his hands were shaking. Rachel was sitting next to him, trying not to show that she was watching him out of the corner of her eye. Would the goblin let go of the precious straw?

Four Special Awards

The tallest goblin dropped the magical sherbet straw and started to rip open the parcel. At once, Rachel picked up the straw and handed it to Shelley. It shrank to fairy size at once, and she tucked herself into Kirsty's bag.

"Sherbet straws!" the goblin exclaimed when he found his prize. "Yummy."

He had already forgotten about the magical straw. While the goblins continued with their game, the girls slipped away and went back to Anna's party.

As they walked in, they could see the fizzy green mess on the floor had vanished. All the sweets were back in their bowls, the tablecloth was back on the table and the hall looked clean and tidy again. Even the balloons were bobbing neatly in groups of red, blue, green and yellow.

"Lovely!" said Rachel, and the other

children nodded happily.

"Hey, everyone, guess what?" said
Kirsty. "My Aunt Harri is going to be
here soon with a big surprise."

"Here she comes!," said Rachel,
glancing out of the window.

Shelley dived back into Kirsty's bag.
A few seconds later, Aunt Harri came
into the hall, carrying a huge cake box.

While Anna and all her guests sat down,
giggling, the girls helped to lift the cake
out of the box. It had two iced layers,
with stars and an enormous sherbet
candy flying saucer on the top. Special
candles spelled out Anna's name.

"It's perfect," said Kirsty.

They watched as Aunt Harri lit the

candles. Then Rachel and Kirsty lifted the cake together and carried it towards Anna, singing *Happy Birthday*. All the other children joined in. Anna's mouth fell open in amazement when she saw the incredible cake.

"This is a special birthday surprise from Candy Land," said Rachel.

"You've been chosen to receive a
Candy Land Helping Hands award,"

Kirsty added. "They
want to thank you for
all your hard work,
and all the money
you have raised
for the children's
hospital."

"Happy birthday,
Anna!" everyone
cheered.

The rest of the
Helping Hands
award winners, Ori,

Olivia and Tal, gathered around Anna,
hugging her and smiling.

"Congratulations, Anna," said Ori,
smiling at her. "You really deserve it."

"I'm so honoured," said Anna, with happy tears in her eyes. "Thank you. The cake looks incredible."

"How do you feel?" asked Mrs Goldman.

Anna looked around at her friends' smiling faces, her pile of presents and her wonderful cake.

"Getting presents and prizes is lovely," she said. "But the best feeling comes from helping people."

"I agree," said Olivia. "Three cheers for Anna!"

All the children cheered as Anna went to cut the cake. Then each guest was given a scrumptious slice.

"Yum," said Rachel after her first bite.

"It's delicious – and it's got just the right amount of fizz."

When the cake had been eaten up, Mrs Goldman clapped her hands to get everyone's attention.

"It's time for a treasure hunt," she said.

"There are twenty packets of sherbet flying saucers hidden in the back garden. It's your job to find them all."

Everyone charged towards the door. Giggling, Rachel and Kirsty ran to join in, but Shelley popped her head out of Kirsty's bag.

"Wait a moment," she said. "It's almost time for the Harvest Feast in Fairyland. Do you still want to come? Don't forget, time will stop in the human world while you're in Fairyland, so no one will notice that you've been gone."

Rachel and Kirsty held hands and exchanged an excited smile.

"We'd love to come," said Rachel.

Shelley waved her wand, and the girls disappeared in a flurry of magical sparkles.

The Harvest Feast

Rachel and Kirsty blinked as the
sparkles faded. They were standing in the
middle of the Sweet Factory orchard in
Fairyland, and it was filled with happy,
busy fairies flitting to and fro. Long tables
were set up around the orchard, laden
with wicker baskets of sweets.

"It looks as if the candy harvest went well," said Rachel with a smile.

"Everyone has been busy harvesting the delicious sweets ready for today," said Shelley with a smile. "Oh look, there are the other Candy Land Fairies. Monica! Lisa! Gabby! I've got my magical sherbet straw back!"

The other fairies zoomed towards Shelley, Rachel and Kirsty and threw their arms around them, twirling around in a big fairy hug.

"We knew that Rachel and Kirsty could help," said a gentle voice.

It was Queen Titania. She and King Oberon had appeared beside them. The fairies fluttered apart and curtsied.

"We are delighted to have you here as our special guests," said King Oberon. "Thank you for helping the Candy Land Fairies. We wouldn't be having today's feast if it weren't for you."

"We are so happy that we could help," said Kirsty.

The queen began to speak, but her voice was drowned out by a tremendous clap of thunder. Jack Frost appeared in a flash of blue lightning.

"How am I supposed to have a sweet shop at my castle without any sweets?" he demanded, jabbing his bony finger at Rachel and Kirsty. "It's all your fault!"

"You only wanted the sweets so you could eat them all yourself," said Kirsty.

"Besides, you

were stealing sweets from everyone else," Rachel added. "That was naughty."

"Yah boo sucks to you," said Jack Frost, blowing a loud raspberry at them.

Queen Titania stepped forward, a serious look on her face.

"The Harvest Feast is supposed to be a happy and welcoming event," she said. "You were wrong to steal the magical sweets, and you were wrong to be rude to our special guests. But if you can promise to behave yourself, we would like you to join our feast."

Jack Frost scowled, but then he saw all the sweets in the baskets and nodded.

"Good," said King Oberon. "Then let the feasting begin!"

The Harvest Feast was one of the best parties that the girls had ever known. Gabby held a biggest-bubble competition with bubble gum, Monica organised a marshmallow-and-spoon race, and

Lisa ran a guess-the-jelly-bean-flavour competition. Rachel and Kirsty especially loved the fizzy party punch that Shelley made with sherbet. They laughed, played and danced among the candy trees until the stars were twinkling in the sky. Then Shelley put her arms around their waists.

"I wish you didn't have to leave," she said. "But it's time for you to go and enjoy the other party now."

Kirsty and
Rachel gave
the Candy
Land
Fairies one
last hug
goodbye,
and then
Shelley
waved her
wand. Suddenly
they found themselves running
into the Wetherbury village hall garden
to join the treasure hunt.

"I'm glad we haven't missed a second
of Anna's party," said Kirsty. "But I
don't mind if we don't find any candy
treasure."

"I agree," said Rachel, laughing.

"Sweets are best as a special treat – and I think I ate enough in Fairyland!"

Soon it was time to go home. Anna gave the girls each a party bag and a balloon as they left.

"Thank you for a lovely party," said Rachel, hugging her. "Happy birthday!"

In Aunt Harri's van, the girls peeped
inside their party bags.

"Yum, lots of
sherbet sweets,"
said Kirsty.
"I'm going to
share mine
with Mum
and Dad
when I get
home."

"Good idea,"
said Rachel. "I'm
too full up to eat any more sweets today!
Oh look, there's something else as well."

She pulled out a large tube of sherbet
that said 'Thank you' along the side, in
glittery gold writing.

"How strange," said Aunt Harri. "I

helped Anna's mum fill the party bags,
and I don't remember putting those in."

Kirsty and Rachel exchanged a secret
smile. They knew that it was a magical
message from their fairy friends.

"I'm so glad we were able to help," said
Kirsty in a low voice. "Now the Candy
Land Fairies can make sure that all
candy is sweet and delicious. Didn't we
have fun? I wonder when we'll see our

fairy friends again."

"Soon, I hope," said Rachel. "Having magical adventures makes me feel as fizzy as sherbet!"

The End

Now it's time for Kirsty and
Rachel to help ...

Samira the Superhero Fairy

Read on for a sneak peek ...

"I love absolutely everything about summer," said Kirsty Tate, who was skipping down Tippington High Street with her best friend Rachel Walker. "I love the sunshine and the long days – and most of all I love you staying with me for a whole week. We're going to have so much fun."

"I can't stop smiling," said Rachel. "I'm so excited about this film."

The girls were on their way to Tippington's little cinema. It was showing the brand-new summer blockbuster *Dragon Girl and Tigerella*, starring the girls' favourite superheroes.

"I can't wait to find out what adventures Dragon Girl and Tigerella are going to have," said Kirsty. "It's going to be amazing to see them in a film together – that's never happened before."

"What do you like best about them?" asked Rachel.

"I like the way Dragon Girl flies through the sky so fast when she's going to save someone," said Kirsty. "It reminds me of our fairy friends when they want to help human beings."

"I love seeing Tigerella use her super strength," said Rachel. "Do you remember when she lifted a whole bus of schoolchildren with just one hand? She's so cool."

"The best part is that they have normal lives too, just like us," said Kirsty. "It's only when danger strikes that they become superheroes and go to help people. I wish I had a secret identity."

Rachel squeezed her best friend's hand.

"You do, in a way," she said. "After all, no one else knows that we are friends of Fairyland."

Just then, they heard a faint mew.

"That sounded like a cat," said Kirsty, looking around.

They were standing beside a high garden fence with a cherry tree inside. As Kirsty looked at the tree, she saw a ball of black fluff clinging to one of the branches. A pair of scared eyes peered at her through the petals.

"It's a kitten," she said. "I think it's stuck. We should go and tell the people who live here."

The kitten gave another sad mew and

Rachel tried to open the garden gate.

"It's locked," she said. "They must be out. What are we going to do? We can't just leave the poor kitten here."

She looked up and down the high street, hoping to see a grown-up to ask for help. But it was a quiet day in Tippington, and there was no one in sight.

Read **Samira the Superhero Fairy** to find out what adventures are in store for Kirsty and Rachel!

Calling all parents, carers and teachers!
The Rainbow Magic fairies are here to help
your child enter the magical world of reading.
Whatever reading stage they are at, there's
a Rainbow Magic book for everyone!
Here is Lydia the Reading Fairy's guide to
supporting your child's journey at all levels.